TINYRANNOSAURUS
AND THE
NEVERSAURUS

By
Nick Ward

Albury Children's

Tinyrannosaurus (wrecks) loves his bedtime stories, and because he is the fiercest little dinosaur ever, he especially likes **SCARY** stories.

The scarier the better!

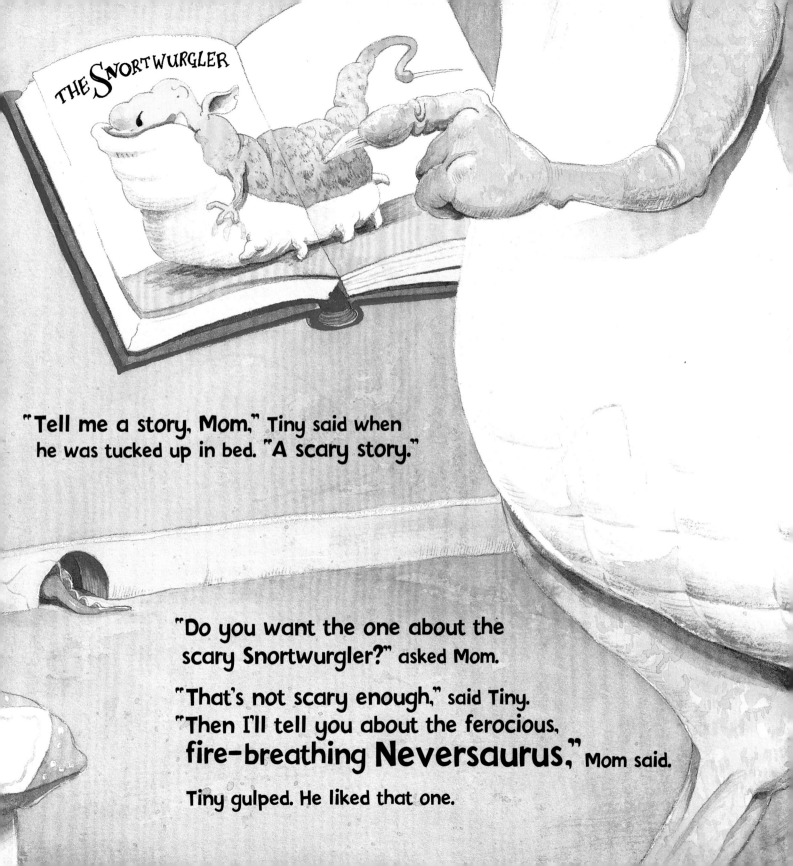

THE SNORTWURGLER

"Tell me a story, Mom," Tiny said when he was tucked up in bed. "A scary story."

"Do you want the one about the scary Snortwurgler?" asked Mom.

"That's not scary enough," said Tiny. "Then I'll tell you about the ferocious, fire-breathing **Neversaurus**," Mom said.

Tiny gulped. He liked that one.

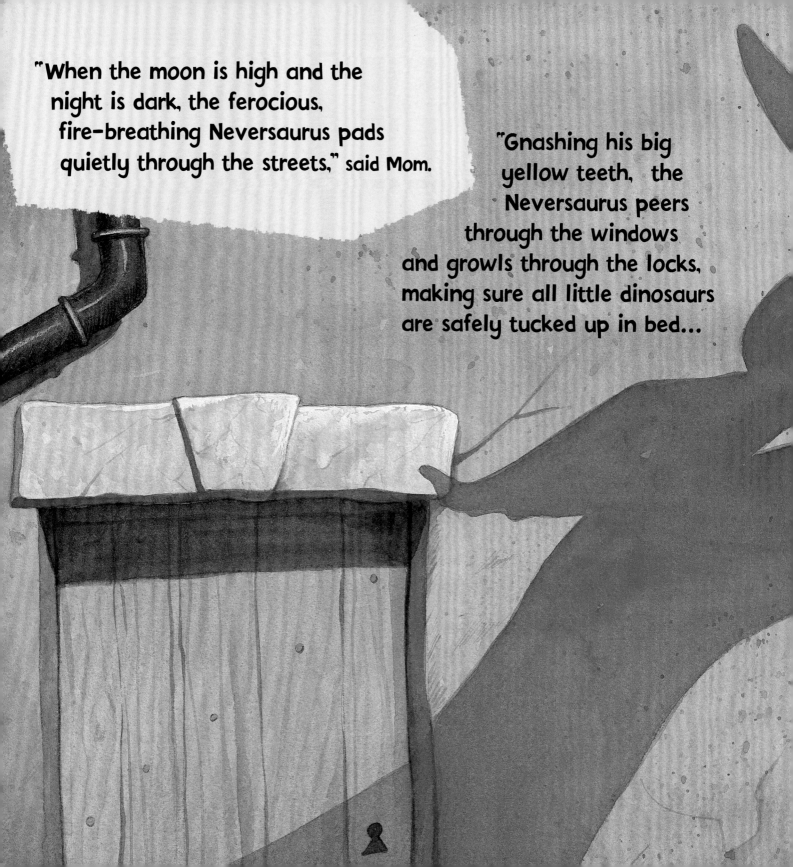

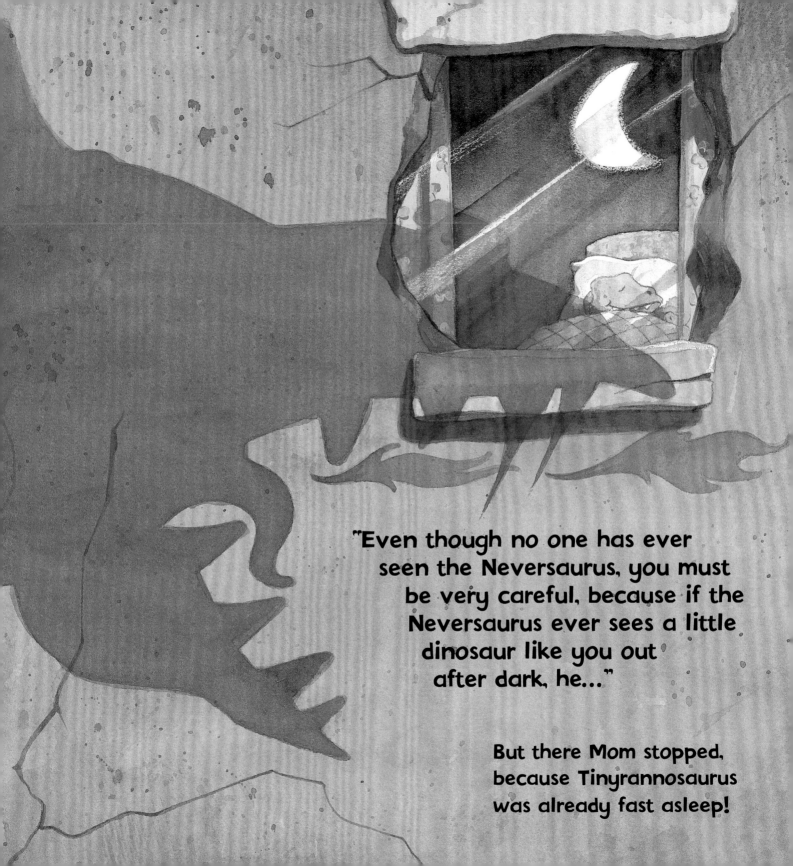

"Even though no one has ever
seen the Neversaurus, you must
be very careful, because if the
Neversaurus ever sees a little
dinosaur like you out
after dark, he..."

But there Mom stopped,
because Tinyrannosaurus
was already fast asleep!

Early the next morning, Tiny made some sandwiches, got out his biggest fishing net and marched into the garden. "Where are you going?" asked Mom.

"I'm going to catch that ferocious, **fire-breathing Neversaurus**," said Tiny.

"**Well, make sure you are back in time for dinner,**" smiled Mom.

Tinyrannosaurus wasn't scared of anything and he roared his loudest roar as he tiptoed through the jewel bright jungle, fishing net at the ready.

"This is just the sort of place to find a Neversaurus," he thought.

And then, he heard a noise coming from the undergrowth. A rumbling, wheezing noise.

Tiny swung his net. "**Got you,** you horrible Neversaurus," he growled.

But...

"Oh Tiny," said Baby Kong.
"I was having my nap."

"Sorry I caught you napping," said Tiny.
"But I'm hunting the ferocious,
fire-breathing **Neversaurus.**"

"I'll help," said Baby Kong,
and they roared their loudest roars
and pulled their fiercest faces
and went on their way.

"This is just the sort of place to find a Neversaurus," whispered Tiny as they tiptoed up to the edge of the bubbling, sulphurous swamp.

"**There he is,**" said Baby Kong, pointing to a large horn sticking out of the mud.

FLOP!

Tiny swung his net. **"Got you, you horrible Neversaurus!"** they bellowed.

"I'll help," said Dinoceros, and they roared their loudest roars and crashed their mighty jaws and went off to find the ferocious, fire-breathing **Neversaurus.**

"We are bound to find the Neversaurus here," said Tiny, after they had waded through the tall, prickly prairie grass and climbed to the top of a boulder.

They looked all around.
"There he is," cried Dinoceros.
Tiny swung his net.

"Oh no! This is ridiculous,"

yelled Tiny, getting very grumpy indeed. All they had caught was a rather dozy Brontosaurus, munching lazily on the grass.
"We'll never find the Neversaurus at this rate."

"Let's climb the big volcano," suggested Baby Kong. "We'll be able to see for miles and miles from there."

So the three friends marched off to the big volcano.

The sun started to set as they looked
out over the valley. They couldn't see
a Neversaurus anywhere.

"Perhaps we should go home," shivered Baby Kong.
"If the Neversaurus finds us out after dark, he'll..."

"I'm not scared of him," said Tinyrannosaurus.
"We've looked everywhere.
**I DON'T BELIEVE THERE IS
SUCH A THING AS A SILLY
NEVERSAURUS,"**
he shouted.

But if only they could see what you can see!

The ferocious Neversaurus
roared his mightiest roar,
blowing plumes of
smoke and coils
of fire into
the air.

"Quick," cried the friends, "The volcano is erupting!" And as the ground shook and the sky filled with flares and flashes and whizz-bangs, they scampered all the way down the hill.

"Good," smiled the Neversaurus. "They should get home in time for dinner."

"Did you find your ferocious, fire-breathing **Neversaurus?**" asked Mom, when Tiny raced into the kitchen.

"No," complained Tiny.

"We never saw the Neversaurus, and the Neversaurus never saw us!"

But we know better,
don't we!

For the very scary,
Mighty Markmilloseros.
Good hunting!

N.W.

First published in 2004 by
Meadowside Children's Books,

This edition published in 2014 by Albury
Books, Albury Court, Albury, Thame,
OX9 2LP, United Kingdom

Text © Nick Ward
Illustrations © Nick Ward
The rights of Nick Ward to be identified as
the author and illustrator have been asserted
by them in accordance with the Copyright,
Designs and Patents Act, 1988

ISBN 978-1-909958-50-0 (hardback)
ISBN 978-1-909958-29-6 (paperback)

A CIP catalogue record for this
book is available from the British Library
10 9 8 7 6 5 4 3

Printed in China